LINE TO NIGHT ISLAND

by the same author

novels

LOS ANGELES, or AMERICAN PHARAOHS

MY NAME IS DEE

FIGHTING DOWN INTO THE KINGDOM OF DREAMS

feature films

A WILDERNESS IN YOUR HEART

PARTY GAMES

AMERICAN MESSENGER

Line to Night Island

ROBIN WYATT DUNN

Published by
JOHN OTT

San Diego

First Published 2014

This book was published in the United States of America while it still existed. This document is in your hands and you are reading this while the world spins about you and you are ours, and we are yours, in Night Island and elsewhere, a tribe in night without a name, but with no ill designs on you, Gentle Reader. This is a story told for you by one of yours, wherever we may be, and whenever, we are connected: in the bonds of words and stars, limitless horizons—

Cover art by Barbara Sobczyńska

ISBN 978-1-940830-00-1

Learn more about the author at www.robindunn.com

for Sarah

"Full of wonder at so strange a form of madness,
they flocked to see it from a distance."

—*Cervantes*

Chapter 1 - Awake

I hold the beacon in my hand, shining up into the sky. Its signal is religious in intensity, mutant freak sanctuary night, limpid circle summoning the thirst for meaning, inside the cavity of my skull my holy roar is culled and cooled and caught mapped spiked like the beacon in my hand, shining in the sky.

It's Power Rangers; it's Thundercats. Ho!

Thundercats, ho, baby, but listen to what I'm gonna tell you now:

This wasn't the first time, and it won't be the last, because we have entered Night Island.

I got a line baby but it ain't gonna hold for long, so jump on with your friends, jump on and rock this whale road with your wishes, it's a long way down (to Earth)—

- -

My hand is lit, huge and white, like a fish. That's how it seems, because it's so dark here by the lighthouse on the rocks. The beacon is a white streaming phosphorous dream.

If I would speak, I could say:

Well. What could I say. There aren't any words that are right; it's too immense.

Finally I turn it off. I head back to the lighthouse, strapping the beacon into the bed of the boat, listening to the sky, as I row, listening for what I might have summoned.

A summoning is raw, and I'm a raw foodist in this way: experience unmollified, and my neighbors are Villains, I know them well. I am Uncle but I am under every standing face, I am an aspect of you.

- -

The truth is that I'm still learning the place myself. It has so many meanings I can sense behind the things I see, and every one of them is real, and true. But, just like on Earth, here on Night Island there is a limited field of truth, too, pick any truth you like but it's got to fall into that window, that limited limitless that is the sky of your mind. That is you and yours and the world.

The lighthouse has no light in it, which is why I have the beacon, but the lighthouse is tall, and, you might say, righteous, because the lighthouse in its mood and spirit invites sensible behavior and wholesome friendships, tasty dinners and good conversation. It is that kind of place, in spite of the fact that it borders on Nightmare, it is good.

- -

I saw her rowing north and I thought: *my god, look at that hair.* I'm only a man, it's what I saw, her red hair. On Earth, I might have thought, O, *not another redhead,* but here those sentiments don't have meaning, here we are not reducible to our stereotypes; here every action has a meaning and every person is full of action, like a dream, only realer.

- -

I felt one of the Villains in the sky, like a brother, as I set to water again, north from my lighthouse, seeking the woman I had seen, but more than that—

Mapping the territory. Who knows when I can again return?

- -

Night Island has no proper name. It has no proper habits. It is more wit than writing, and more wail than whale; it is tiny. It speaks, a music you may have heard, only listen:

- -

I sail under sea by gobbets of the city that was nuked inside my fever I am fine but outside it I am raging on a mountain of desire and flaking skin that is the old me, that is the one I was, that was the Lighthouse Keeper.

Once I kept a lighthouse with no light but now I sail north without a sail and I am free. Freedom, the end of the earth, the beginning of the serpent wheel, ourobourous urge my oars—bore my ears to hear the rearing fears who fill my eyes!

Synethesthesia is a meal. Yummy yummy—

Stroke. Stroke, Stroke. I smell the woman on the breeze.

- -

A redhead but north is where the women live; they make the rules. But now I know the Villain is yet further north, beyond their purview, for they make no rules for Villains, I see the map inside my mind:

- -

What was the lighthouse? What was it I was keeping? And where am I bound?

On the shore approaching:

I see her hair again in this not-light without source musicking wiles onto the map of her flaming head enraging taming my man's heart my eyes driven wicked and divine—

She is stepping off her boat. I can see, a mile distant, a storm coming.

- -

Widgets crickets and the mad moon, this storm is a fragment—

[tell time tell a lie tell me where you were when I had to die, for I am dead and this is history, this is the time you made me sob because it was the truth and because it was in my eye, the speaking burg, a suburb rube and cutting herb is where you'll go when we have laid the wax out on your face to doppelganger make embrace his race is your race and this time is your time lay me out fine etherized baby I am your patient on the table of the sky and I will will it now to die, this face who is the universe—

and in our death we'll cut your body like a package of potato chips and rip it open to deserve our just desserts inside the country of the mind, on a lone highway—]

The storm is slow, and I grip the boat's sides, waiting for the light to pass.

Night Island rocks me.

- -

LINE TO NIGHT ISLAND

I got a line but it's slow, and kind of fizzy, tell me, can you hear it? Let me touch your face.

- -

The town is deserted when I arrive; no sign of anyone, and the firelight of her hair and the firelight of the world she brought out of the air is gone too. But I can smell her, over the sand and water, over the heath.

The heath.

The heath, my god. I am estuary inside my body, liver, toenail, placenta—

I am estuary inside this dark universe:

I am flowing north.

The heath is speaking to me.

I must be silent.

- -

[ ]

- -

I am in the heath

- -

I am Dun and I am War; I am Bright And I am Glory;

I am Dark Island.

I am Dark Island in Night Island and I am lonely—

- -

I am in the heath! I am startling fast! I am this face of wax who died!

Hear me!

(

She hears me.)

- -

Man! (she says)

Fetch me a stone! (she says)

(and I do)

Toss it! (she says)

(and I do)

The stone is warped and old, a dun thing for a dun world—

I am Lisle she says.

I am Dun, I say.

Catch me if you can, she says.

And I am running.

- -

In the heath there is no memory. And there is no undoing. Everything you do is done and it can never be undone; it is incorruptible.

LINE TO NIGHT ISLAND

It is written in the book of life. It is marked into your soul and into the souls of others, carved into the flesh and blood and ouroubous of the coursing Morse of particlestuff—

I am a man I'm running

Wait! (I say)

She is laughing.

I can feel the Villain o'er the sky.

I can feel the purple in my eye, covered on the heather, covered on the sky my heart is wild and it is an orbiting globe so far away that its gravity does not describe our selves any longer—

I am too far away!

(Wait!) she says.

(Where are you!) I say.

(Over here!) she says.

But I do not see her.

But I can hear her.

(I'm right here) she says.

(Where are you?) I say.

(Right here) she says, next to my ear.

But she is only wind.

- -

Inside the Dark Island of myself I am welling horrendous things, they well out of my skin, my kin is weeping in my history, making me sweat.

I wipe it off but it keeps coming; history.

I want to shout for her again but I know she's gone. Nor did the Villain get her either; she's just gone. I can still smell her, but she's far.

Here in the heath I am lonely. It is a cold loneliness of much comfort, you settle in to wait (in the stars) in the cold heather, the moisture flowing over your face, like god, like music, it is an order, fragrance, and message that is borne to you by many, on an order of one, ordinal divine, your body:

MESSENGER

(the voice says)

MESSENGER, AWAKE

(I am awake, I say)

MESSENGER, A MESSAGE

(What is it, I say)

LONG AGO WE KNEW A SONG BUT WE HAVE FORGOT. WHEN WE FORGOT IT WAS A MUSIC OF FORGETTING, SO WE TRY TO REMEMBER THAT FORGETTING WHAT IT MEANT WHAT IT FELT WHEN IT WAS GONE AND WE SUSPECT THAT YOU ARE THAT FORGETTING, THAT YOU ARE COME TO WIPE US CLEAN.

(I know nothing but that everything we do is written in the sky), I say, (That is how it always was and how it's always been and to be otherwise would be heresy, but more, it would be wrong, why would you have the universe forget your time?)

YOUR LOVE IS A MESSAGE

I fall asleep, forgetting the message, in the cold and in the damp.

In Night Island the line is welting but the line is warm, and the line is telling because the line is yours, it wills and whirls for your delight, to speak the name you have been hearing—

The women are come. I was dreaming but I have awoken again; they carry me out of the heath; out of the rain. In the purple heather I am a potato sack and they're myriad Nereids, sea women on the stone earth, swimming—

(Where is she?) I say.

(Shhhh) they say.

- -

The women are officious, but kindly so. They tell many stories, between grinding flour and weaving urns. I can hear their children near, but they will not let me see them; I am in an airlock of their security zone, waiting to be cleared.

Under the starred sky, riding on the orb of this isle, I was Lighthouse Keeper boatman, but my *langsam* bears strange fruits that demand some little wyrding, my longing is a message but I can't yet read it—

"Well, what are you going to do now?" one of the women asks.

I smile but can't think of anything to say.

“He's cute, isn't he,” says another.

“Kind of skinny.”

“Well, let's put you to work,” says another, and they do, and I am scraping heath from earth and erecting a small Oal bale, one of their temples, temporary, a bailiwick of vine that will burn before the moon is through—

I'm sweating from my work and they give me watered wine and the light is slow but fast, a green and yellow wash of land and fast ideas, it flows like water o'er the roof of their bailiwick temple and I am laughing and they are chanting and then I'm running, a loaf of bread in my hand, I've had too much of religion, I am headed deeper into Night Island I am Dark Island I am Dun, but where is Lisle?

- -

In Night Island is the sea. We're free to be you and me, that was always true, but we're also we—

- -

(us is a fuss but a necessary one, and we keep trying to make it—)

- -

Under the thunder I chant to myself, to keep my feet going. It's cold and wet, and my jacket is starting to seep through. How do people live here, in this cold darkness?

One of the stars is brighter than the others and I set on to follow it, and I know where I am going, but to go there will be a real bad thing, because where I am going is the touch-off zone, it is a door of light, a little teleporter, a little dimensional gate, and if I go there she'll be there but then I'll have to decide:

Do I stay or do I go?

And if I stay who is else is gonna come?

Who will we be when we are them and they are we and we are cutting off the waxèd mask that stems the tide that rushes through this world? Who will we be if we let them all in?

But perhaps not all will want to come. All these spirits. So many spirits! That would be better.

In a haunted land we still need some living souls.

I can see the rocks up on the headland and I climb the heath-covered slope, my boots sliding back but I keep heading up, sweating, my beard filled with flax and grass.

She's standing on a rock, looking out at something.

"Hey you!" I say. "I know you."

She doesn't say anything.

She's beautiful, like before. But her red hair is dark, and there's no light.

"What is it?" I say.

She says, "Shh."

I listen.

On the horizon is a dawn, but far away, and only sound, a slow chorus, an orchestra that can't decide if it's to start.

There's a light, a thin line of light, and that's you, spun in stars above, over my head, fast fire—

She watches it pass over the sky, a satellite.

I put my hand onto her face.

- -

In the many days that I spent on the water I had thought:

What if she kisses me?

And,

What if I am dead?

And,

What if I am dead when she kisses me?

- -

I am an ocean in a stone and my memory is a drone that will not stop outdoing all I do, it's the memory of this rue I threw away but keeps coming back, the memories have stayed and they have stayed and they keep speaking.

- -

She's still standing there.

"Who are you?" she says.

"My name is Dun," I say. "Don't you know me?"

But she shakes her head and goes down to her hut.

“What is it?” I say.

She waves me away, and goes inside her hut. I sit outside it.

People are crazy.

The dawn is still going on and sounds more raucous now; it's no longer an orchestra but more a brawl, an ugly one. It is distant.

This near darkness and the few stars are warm; the one I followed has set but I can almost feel it. I hear the woman rustling in her hut, and she comes out with cheese, and I split the rest of my bread with her and we eat it in the cold.

“Where did you come from?” she says.

“From the Lighthouse.” I say. “I saw you there.”

She doesn't say anything to that.

I finish chewing my food and watch her chewing, watch her eyes. She's far away still, thinking.

“This is a lonely spot here,” I say. She nods.

“How long have you been here?” I ask her.

- -

This is a memory but it is an untrue one. I felt her there then, but looking deeply in her eyes was a mistake; it isn't often that way, but it was then, because then—

- -

The Gate had Arrived.

There are many Gates and many corridors and as a Lighthouse Keeper (though I have no light) I know many of them, and this is a grave one, a mighty one, a dangerous one, bright brilliant blue, shot like a rifle through the stone and earth and sky, like the spindle of a gyroscope, or an arrow through an eye.

qqq

The Gate was Light and it was blue, fired from the sky and through the hillock in the dark of Night Island, by Lisle's hut.

I stood and took a few steps towards it but she grabbed my arm, and I looked at her, and it was like she was pleading with me.

"We have to greet them," I said. Whoever they are.

She tore her hair and screamed and ran around her hut, but she didn't leave, and I didn't move, just waited, watching her, watching the Gate hum, watching the sky.

(And what if it is a Villain that comes? Well, they're not so bad. They're temporary.)

- -

It wasn't as bad as I thought. I only had to sing a song, and she helped. You have to make the spirits go away; you can't live with all of them. The Gate sings and it goes; I remember that now.

When I was a child I was already a messenger; I know that now. For though we are angels we are slow, and the messages we bear are worlds, they need water and air and light and we're slow to carry them, over so many rivers on the backs of so many horses my woman bears my child but is the earth a message or is my message the earth I wear a black hat but I am good but my eyes are dark and the sky is red.

LINE TO NIGHT ISLAND

When I was a child I was already dead; this life is what came after.

In the storm I held her, my self; she was crying.

- -

In Night Island we are waiting for your visit. I cry a fatal music for your children; I am singing now.

Chapter 2 - The Gas Station

I've got you, lover, and I'm sorry about that. But my son is born and he has a yellow sun; he has a yellow sun.

I'm here and I'm a daddy but I got a briefcase and inside it are my instructions:

- -

In Night Island I am humming, I am humming with my wife. We are humming, we are humming to the dark sun.

I can spin my son around, holding onto his arms, but what happens when I have to go?

I am still this goddamned knight on contract; I am still Parsifal of sorts, on a quest without a name and without a by-your-leave or what-you-will, it's slavery by other means, and the means they are your stars—

Your stars have drenched me in and I am choking by the bin inside our kitchen, waiting for the light to go out of the night.

"It's gonna be okay, honey," my wife says. I hate the beginning of a quest.

- -

I am riding. I am riding in the midst of everything because my horse just had to get it in, that it is smarter than I am. He's made of light—

- -

Coursing yellow red and white, the saddle is a bite into the fabric of the seams we see along the edges of the barn that is the universe; it's only a bit of weaving...

(don't look too close at what seeps through the edges)

- -

Say Hallelujah, I am come, I am Parsifal, but my name is Dun. I am Dark Island from Night Island but my words are gum, and I will stick 'em underneath your desk when you're not looking.

I'm here from the government. And I'm here to help. Behold my sword, my pen.

Lady, have you heard here of a quest?

"What in the devil are you on about?" she says, tending to her daffodils, they smile enraptured at her bulbous face, they wait for water like they wait for death; with shining daffodillian teeth...

"My quest is not from the Devil, of that I can assure you, lady, I am here on the Business of Government and God and I can say it is most serious, except I'm not quite sure, to tell the truth, just what it is..."

"Well, then, get out of my face, goddamn it!"

"Yes ma'am..."

I have a steed it's made of light, now if I could only find my mind...

I have a son with a yellow sun but I am afraid. What if something should happen? Will my son know all he needs? Will I know when the quest is over?

I have a son with a yellow star; he flies above my eyes.

"Hey, Lady!"

"What!"

"Where can a knight find a quest around here?"

"Try over at the gas station."

- -

The gas station is long gone, along with the gas, but the attendant stays...attending on God, I suppose.

"Hail, traveler!" I say, dismounting from my smart-aleck mount.

The man is sad because, as I can see, he has a head half in another world, a world that's departing, or perhaps already has, it swirls about his face in a penumbra of the glad and righteous furor of fading civilizations...

"Sir, I'm told you know of quests! My name is Dun, I am a Parsifal sort of Knight, from Night Island. Can you help?"

"Yes, I know of one," he says.

"What is it?" I say.

"I am a bed," he says. "I have no eyes."

I listen to the man. Quests are known to begin this way; you listen to it and it takes you o'er the sea, over the lap of grandpa, for the punishment you've earned...

"In my blindness I have seen the coming of a sword," the man says, "over the galaxies. It rants and raves but its transmission is quite clear to me. It is a sword and it is talking; it has been talking for days. It insists you're not of this universe, and that you'll know the password that it seeks, a nursery rhyme it's craved now for many an age, it is melancholy as a mad king, made of steel..."

"Aye, sir. And where can I find this melancholy sword?"

"Why, I have it right here," he says, puts his dagger quick at my neck. I have been fooled. But then the gas station attendant keeps on talking, and I'm not sure whether the sound is blade or man:

"I knew you were a wizard the moment I laid eyes on you; I knew it. I knew it true. So here's what I'm gonna do. I'm gonna kill you good and dead but first I'm gonna use you for my own fell purposes, which include: The Tel Aviv Tableau Vivante."

I smile, with the steel right at my jugular. Nodding seems a bad idea; he smiles back at me.

"The Tel Aviv Tableau Vivante I always wanted to see, and now I can. Stand over there, knight, and hold your sword up in the air; I'll watch your horse for you. Go on now."

And so I back away real slow; I can't abandon my trusty steed, and stand over by the unleaded pumps, rusted half away, and raise my blade into the sky; she towers over me, my wife, my boy away, I am a gloomy sort of man, it's why I came...

He takes his picture and uploads it to his mainframe, smiling all the while. I stand steady, in case he wants a second shot, but after several minutes none's forthcoming. Do I lower down my arm and rest my blade against my leg?

I am Tableau Vivante; I represent some Fertile Crescent Nonsense, from Old Earth; from the dreams I have; I am a bad knight.

"Sir!" I say. "What about—"

But then it hits me. And it hits him. Light white run hot over the land, I can't even think—

- -

It is an ocean of light; or rather, a tsunami of it. It is a white light flood, blinding psychotropic and I can't hardly move but just a step and then a slow another, my armor creaking...

I hear the attendant scream: "The horse is gone!" He's probably having a grand old time, my horse. Always happier than me...

"My name is Dun and I am Parsifal" I cry into the white blindness. "Tell me what to do!"

There is no answer.

At length I find the attendant; huddled behind a rock smoking his pipe, chuckling like mad.

With a clink I sit down by him, and cover my eyes from the light.

- -

Night Island is my home. She is beautiful; she is true. Have you never seen her? Never once? If you had you'd know why I suffer so. Not for her sake alone, no, but for the world that she knows; she is a secret and she tells me secrets, secrets I can never understand, but that I can act...

"Is it over yet?" I ask the attendant.

But he is weeping.

Luckily I'm good at sleeping.

- -

Where is my briefcase? Where are my launch codes?

- -

I am a knight without a horse. Chevalier sans cheval.

I am a useless thing. A story without an end; a city without residents. I need a purpose. But I have a name; perhaps that's purpose enough. I am Dun I am Dark Island, married to Lisle.

The white is fading; the attendant is gone. So are the gas pumps. The world is new; and bright, and long, and empty. I can hear the insects and the leaves. The grey road is my own. I walk.

- -

I sing in my sleep while I walk; I dream of a red ocean. The blood of my enemies, perhaps. Do I have that many enemies? I can't remember. Haven't seen that many people, lately, it's been a long way down to this my wedding day, no, I was married; wait a minute, was I married?

My name is Parsifal; I am a finch; I've gone insane. Help me, will you? Tell me which way is out?

- -

The screaming does no good. If I have no name. If I have no name. Without a name, I am...not nothing, something. Is that the problem? Before I had a name and so I could be nothing. Now I have none and I am becoming something, something I don't like...

- -

The red trees hover over me like friends but they aren't my friends. I know this because they laugh at me as I walk past them except I can't walk past them because they keep hovering over me, their leaves smears of blue blood against the midnight sky, courting the stars. The stars are fruits. My son is there, but he is turning white...

When did I see him last? I am an absentee father; my briefcase the bonus, my ornery absolution the regimentation of empires, my name, my name, my name—

These trees don't know either. I scream at them. I scream at them as loud as I can. But they're only trees.

Snap it together there, buddy. You can figure this one out.

You have some kind of ridiculous armor on; take that off. It's better. To be naked. Now I can think.

Where was I? In a crib? No, with my wife. She held my face in her hands and told me to remember something; get the milk. I need to get the milk. It is a quest. I have no name, but I have a quest. I am a man. I will get the milk.

Where is the milk. It is in the supermarket? Where is that? I do not know. How do I know? I just know. How does one get to the supermarket. I must be Superman, to know the Supermarket, I see that now. And so I fly into the air—

I am screaming. With joy.

Chapter 3 - The Supermarket

"Sir, you're going to have to leave that outside."

The woman, the guard, the employee, in her green awning, I mean her green lipstick, that's not the word either, she's wearing a green thing, over her chest and her thighs, it's called: an awning. I forget.

"I need it. I'm Superman," I say, pointing to my leotard.

"That's very nice, sir," she says, "But Halloween isn't for another few days. You'll frighten the children in that getup, so just leave it out here."

Frightened, I take off the jumpsuit and the red cape and hand it to the guard in her awning. Her lipstick. Whatever that cloth thing is she's wearing with pockets in it. A refrigerator. No that isn't it either.

Anyway. I'm naked in the supermarket. This is progress. They have milk here and I will get some, and then the universe will be saved.

I can almost hear my wife's voice in my head: "..." It's like a metronome, or the tide of the sea. That's what she is, an ocean.

My sword is gone but I still have my hand so I raise it boldly and I charge ahead; into Aisle Five:

- -

Much has occurred. Have you ever been in a supermarket? Its name is accurate; its forces are greater than most universes. It is a miracle I am alive. I fell at its edge and tumbled into space; the edge of its Aisle Five Space was an illusion, designed to trick the unwary, I tumbled in an abyss of time that knew no counting...

But I made it here. They have toothpaste here. I can smell it. But I cannot see it. Kelp. And sugar. Light blue. All around clean teeth. It is so dark here, but it doesn't feel like home. I call out:

"Hello!"

"...ello..."

Milk. I am a purpose; I am aspect of my wife's will. I am knight. That is who I am; knight. I may have no name but I have a purpose. Milk. I stand on my own two legs.

"Milk, where are you!" I cry out into the dark. In the distance, like a small insect, I can hear a cash register. It opens and coins jingle. A receipt spits out its paper with its purple words printed on it. I can hear it, down at the end of the aisle...

"Customer service in Aisle Five" announces a huge voice, somewhere above me, and suddenly I'm surrounded by grinning managers, with hairy arms and pimply faces, gesturing wildly and speaking in a language I cannot understand, something about Tel Aviv brand Matza Castles, I don't understand, I try to indicate that it is milk that I need, that I am on a quest, I am a knight and I serve God, but first my wife, and the baby needs milk, and goddamn it—

I sign whatever's put in front of me. Finally I escape after I agree to wear the Prototype All-Chrome Senior Diaper, Completely Reusable; it shines around my crotch like a distant star...

I am ridiculous. But I was always ridiculous.

And...I remember that I am Knight Parsifal. I have done all this before. It is my meaning; my mission. My mission: meaning. My meaning: a mission. Where is my steed. I wear chrome around my manhood. My helmet and my beard is gone.

I am in a supermarket. I see a young woman.

"Excuse me," I say. "Have you seen any milk?"

"I think it's in Aisle Seventeen," she says.

"Aisle Seventeen? Where is that?"

"Over there," she says, but she points in some direction that I cannot see.

"I'm sorry, where did you say?" and she points again but it is in a direction I cannot see; I see now that she is a higher dimensional being than I am so I will have to take the long way round.

"Thank you, miss," I say, but she is already back examining the cans of green beans.

The hum is greater now and things are coming in to focus; I am a knight amongst many knights. It is a convention. This is the Round Table. I remember now. Here we convene. Here we gather the Holy Vessels, The Grail and all the rest...but I need a briefcase...I'm going to blow something up...

"Excuse me," says a woman, grabbing my arm. "I need your help."

Her eyes are dark pools. Her body, long, and drenched with seawater...

I say nothing, only stare at her. Into her eyes.

"I need a man's opinion," she says. "Is this spatula feminine, would you say?" She holds out the spatula for me to examine, gripped in her white-gloved hand, it writhes a bit in her grip, snapping its neck about, and growling. I pet its gleaming head.

"Very nice," I say. "Tell me, have you seen—"

"My husband left me," she says, leaning closer to me. "I need a new spatula. It's so nice having a man around the supermarket. Tell me, do you shop here often?"

"No, I'm from Night Island..."

"You're a knight, aren't you?" she says.

"Yes..."

"I thought they were all dead."

I walk away, her hand clutching at my arm, her voice retreating behind me, the air grows cooler...I must be approaching a refrigerated section!

I can see it! The refrigerators! Gleaming like dark and gloomy gods, little jewels...

They're just where they're supposed to be. I open the refrigerator and feel the freezing air on my naked face and I smile...

There is one milk left. Homogenized. It will have to do. "They just didn't have any lowfat, honey." This is what I will say. I have to rehearse my lines.

I hold the milk in my hand. I have found it. But now I must return.

- -

I wish I were a wizard with a return spell. But no, I am only a man in the dark, now wearing a chrome-plated reusable diaper. I can't even fly without my leotard.

- -

Two days later I am home. My wife is beside herself; she is screaming. It is why I love her. She can scream louder than the hyenas who attack us here in the summer. The boy has milk. I am Dun. Lisle is my wife. I am alive.

This is Night Island:

We wear our masks. They are death masks. We have our milk. I dance for you:

Here, here now. A sun is born. So far away. Let us salute it in our way, with our bodies. Salutations, great warrior distant, and we dance the Wave, around our fire, and I make the faces for the boy, and my wife is laughing, and howling, with the hyena's blood on her face.

The sun knows us! Tell me, do you know its name?

Chapter 4 - Los Angeles

I am come to you again. The City of Messengers, Los Angeles. I did not want to come here, but here I am. My name is Dun, I am Dark Island from Night Island, married to Lisle, I am Knight Parsifal...but you know all this.

Why am I here. I am on Sunset Boulevard. The Zapato Man is polishing my shoes, in his minivan. The steel greaves shine in his leathered hands.

The yellow light here is so bright—I have gone insane. I remember now.

"Excuse me, sir, is Los Angeles well?"

"Eh?"

"Is the city well? Am I needed?"

"I come from Cuba," he says, smiling. "Done in one moment."

The man does not know. It is not a language difficulty, no, he knows but he will not tell me. So much is known here; this terrible city of knowledge maddens me, I must escape, no. I am only just come. Another quest; I have been recalled, I was reenlisted. My weapon, my words. No, my horse. No, my eyes. No. I have no weapons. Not even my sword.

I must be a sacrifice.

I flee, barefoot down Sunset Boulevard. There are many other barefoot men here.

"Your zapatas!" The Zapato man cries after me. He is after me. They're all after me, here.

I sit down on the iron bench. The bus arrives and the bus conductor leans out of his window to look at me.

"Going somewhere?" he asks me.

"No."

"You're going somewhere. Get on the bus."

"No, I'm staying. I'm staying here," I tell him.

"Get on the bus or I call the police," says the bus conductor.

I consider giving him my ancestry, showing him my heraldry. But the noble lines are lost here, we are in the City of Messengers, and we know no boundaries any longer; or rather the City does not know them, I have *boundaries*, goddamn it, I am a knight!

"I am a knight," I tell him. "Leave me." He sneers but drives on, shooting soot into my face from his bus.

In his wake is a woman, shielding her eyes from the dust. Her scarf is wrapped around her nose; she steps onto the sidewalk and looks at me.

"You're a knight?" she says.

"My name is Dun," I say. "At your service. How may I aid thee?"

"I'm not from around here," she says. "I'm looking for my son..."

“What is your ancestry?” I ask her.

“You’re not from around here either,” she says.

Her eyes are wide but deep too, she is well dressed, and dirty. I can see she is frightened.

“Come, I know where there is water,” I say, and she follows me down the alley to the hose, we take turns slurping from the green rubber.

“Mmm,” she says.

“It is good water in this alley,” I say, “I remember it.”

“It’s been so long since I been to LA,” she says.

“Tell me,” I say. “Who is your son?’

“His name is Andrew. Andrew Bologna. He doesn’t want to see me.”

“Of course he does. You’re his mother. Where is this Andrew Bologna?”

“In Hollywood...”

“West Hollywood?”

“No, Hollywood...“

“North Hollywood?”

“No, Hollywood!”

“This is a problem. I am not allowed in Hollywood.”

"Hey thanks anyway, Mr. Knight, it's been nice chatting with you," the woman says, patting me on my armored shoulder.

"But I will go there, for your sake," I say. "This city has grown strange to me. Perhaps this Bologna knows something about it."

"We can fly," she says, taking out her carpet. The carpet grins at me. I have never gotten along well with carpets, but she's climbing on, and I follow.

The carpet heats up and shakes off its dust, then clutches my ass with sharp teeth and I am howling, without my zapatas, and the woman is screaming with terrible joy and pain and we are in the smog-filled air above Echo Park, flying over Elysian Fields, with the dead Greek warriors calling out their names from the chaparral, as the Dodgers piss over the home plate, we travel West, downwards into the fading Messenger Day, I must leave so soon, so soon, or the city will keep me as its own, and knights are no longer allowed here...

"They let me keep my carpet," she says, tears coming out of her eyes.

We land on the sidewalk in Hollywood.

"That's where he works," she says.

The office complex is dirty, two stories tall, a beaten-down security box emitting angry chirps by the violated gate, chain link swaying in the Santa Ana wind...

"We'd best get inside," I say, and I take the woman's arm and slip through the gap in the chain link, and we hear the security box whisper, "I know you...I know you..."

The building has been freshly painted; an angry dwarf descends the stairs outside the building, cursing at the office he is leaving.

"I'm gonna fuck you up, motherfucker!" he says. He takes out his comb and runs it through his hair; when he sees us he spits onto the grass and goes out through the gate, which hums for him, perhaps some dwarvish mantra.

"Bologna works here?" I ask.

"Yeah, Andrew said he had a job here. But I didn't want to bother him, and then when I called, some woman answered, and she was so weird sounding...I didn't know what to do!"

"Which suite?"

"That one," she says, pointing to a dingy little door with suits standing outside it, smoking.

These are the knights of Los Angeles. These messengers of old. With their Croatian signatories, the ties on their necks, old Montenegro, speak to me:

We walk over to the suits.

"The Halloween Party's across town," says a big black suit, his tie loose but his hair huge, pick in his hair, his teeth gleaming. "You workin' here?"

"This lady is looking for her son," I say. "Andrew Bologna." They all laugh.

"Bologna ain't seein' anybody right now, but you can wait, we're all waiting." The suits smile at us and I reach for my sword, but then remember that it isn't there. I remember that I am a wanted man in Hollywood.

"We'll just knock and see," I say. The big black suit catches my arm as I reach for the door. "You don't want to do that, buddy," he says.

"Let go of my arm," I say. He holds on to it.

"My name's Henry," he says. "Believe me, you don't want to go through that door right now."

"Why not."

"Hang around long enough, and you'll see."

"We haven't got much time," I say. "I'm not allowed here."

"I understand," Henry says, releasing my arm. "You got a nice lady friend there. Look, why don't we get some coffee. There's a decent place down the street."

I look up at the sky and the wind is howling, the sky turning red.

"What about Andrew?" the woman says.

"This man says he can help us," I tell her, and we start back towards the gate.

At the gate Henry does a little breakdance, taking the cardboard out of his pocket, and the gate keeps insisting:

"That is not the way. That is NOT the way, that is NOT THE WAY," but the breakdancing seems to keep it calm, and I do some beat-boxing for Henry, until the gate finally shuts up and opens up to let us back onto the street.

"I hate that motherfucker" Henry whispers.

Down the street I can see the cafe. Yellow lights advertise "COFFEE" in welcoming letters. The wind increases and one of the café chairs is borne aloft, flying towards us and I shield the woman with my armor; it hits me with a crash and the woman lets out a little shriek.

We lean against the wind and make our way to the coffee shop door. I can smell the coffee inside. We go through the door.

My name is Dun and I am Knight Parsifal but I must leave soon. Soon I will not be able to leave Los Angeles; I promised my gods that I would not leave Night Island; I have a child...

“Three lattes,” says Henry, and he takes out a gold coin and spits on it, rubbing off the invisible grime.

The clerk accepts the coin, dropping it into his pocket. “Three lattes,” the clerk says.

- -

We are sitting in the dark red leather booth.

“Bologna has gotten into pornography,” says Henry.

“In Hollywood?” I say. “That’s the Valley.”

“Not just any pornography. French pornography. Intellectual.”

“What?” says the woman.

“Someone offered him a lot of money. Do some twisted ass shit with Jacques Derrida and French ticklers, some kind of foreign soundtrack, I don’t fuckin’ know, but he’s got buyers lined up, you understand? They are *lined up*.”

“In Hollywood.”

“Yeah, man, I know. But it’s intellectual. It’s not soft core, it’s not hard core. It’s French. I think it gets through the zoning restrictions,” Henry says.

“That is fucked up,” I say.

“Not my Bologna!” says the woman.

"You work for Bologna?" I ask Henry.

"No. I don't. I can't tell you who I work for. Anyway, most of the time I work for myself. Like you, man. You're self-employed, right?"

"I serve God."

"Yeah, whatever. Look, you want to get in and see Andrew, you got his moms all here, I get that. But as a friend, okay, I am *advising* you: just go home. Call him tomorrow. You do not want to go into that office. It is not a good office for you and your lady friend to be in right now, okay. You know as well as I do that...well, anyway. Finish your latte. Consider this my friendly warning."

"I am a knight," I say. "I am sworn to—"

But the woman cuts me off. "It's okay, Sir Knight. The thing is, I haven't been completely honest with you."

She adjusts her hair.

"See, I kind of knew about this French porn thing already. The people who tried to take my carpet away, it was them I found about it from. If you ask me, this porno ain't French. It's from Hell."

"From Hell?" I ask.

She nods. "Right off Fairfax," she says, her eyes intense.

"I got to go," says Henry. "This is my number." He slides his card across the table and I put it in my empty scabbard.

"Thanks Henry."

"We have to go to Hell," she says to me.

"Off Fairfax," I say.

"Right at the edge of Beverly Hills."

- -

In the Los Angeles night the freaks no longer come out; the new regime has forbade them their howls and it is so quiet that I can hear the blood in my ears and the hot wind makes my face a stale pancake.

We find the stairwell outside 8383 Wilshire, at the edge of Beverly, and the woman whispers the password in the statue's ear, who raises its halberd to let us pass.

I am Parsifal. The thought is like food, as I descend into the underworld.

Photographs of Jacques Derrida, the French Deconstructionist, cover the brick walls. A snappy secretary with devil horns greets us at the glass doors; we're in the antechamber of Hell, its own jurisdiction, private security stands in the alcoves, smoking clove cigarettes.

"We're here to see Jacques," says the woman, and the secretary pushes a button and a corpse is raised from out her desk, its flesh putrid and grey, but still recognizable as the man on all the posters.

The corpse sits erect on its metal scale, naked and scabby, its limbs discolored. Its eyes are closed. It still has hair on its head.

"I speak for Jacques," says the secretary. "He doesn't do a lot of talking these days. What can I help you folks with?"

"We're here about the porno—" I start, but the woman hushes me.

"We were hoping to get a meeting about a project we've been working on," the woman says. "There's talent attached, and I think Hell would be really interested in our message—"

"We're not taking on any new projects now, I'm sorry," says the secretary, and she reaches for the button to put Jacques back in his grave.

"Wait," I say. "This corpse. You worship it?"

The secretary looks at me with her strange eyes.

"He is avatar," she says, in a quiet voice. In an alcove, one of the security puts out his cigarette.

"I am avatar also," I say, and then the security are pulling out their guns. The woman lets out a little shriek.

"Let me touch the man," I say, and I reach for Derrida's neck.

I am a power but I am alone; if I fetch your sun, son, be with me, for I am alone—and I am a vengeance—

Jacques's eyes open onto darkness, and his mouth widens.

A bug crawls out from between his lips.

I clutch the corpse's neck.

"Speak," I say. More bugs crawl from out its mouth, and then the corpse is coughing, and it spits out a dozen of them, chewed into a quivering mass.

"Eckkgh," says the corpse.

"You are dead and I am alive, Jacques. I am come to you on a quest from God, and I will have your answer to my questions or I will deliver fire to all of your family, now, and in the future, for as many generations as I exist. Do you understand me, Frenchman?"

I can almost see a tear in his eye.

"*Je comprends.*"

"This woman's son has been corrupted by your evil. Your French evil. But it is not even French. It is your own. I will have you release Andrew Bologna from your evil. Unbind him."

"*Mais il est venu parce qu'il voulait*...he came, because he wanted to—"

I lean into the corpse's stinking face.

"These people call you avatar. But you are a corpse. You have no gifts. You are dead. All that was yours is now taken from you, but you live on in this half-life. Would you have me release you? Perhaps Bologna did come to you freely, but he was not free enough. Not as long as you exist..."

"He exists because we *want him to exist,* Knight," said the Secretary. "I think it's time for you to leave. You can leave on your feet, or on your back."

I reach for my sword but it is not there, only Henry's business card.

I am a dancer. Before the first avatar descended from the line of Vishnu to spin the universe into its Hindu light, I was on my horse and I was a *mensch* with a hotcake inside me and a mountain on my ass, I have got the moves that will hurt you, because they are so sad.

I take the security with my hands and with my dancing that can know no telling. The secretary flees through the glass doors, deeper into Hell, and the woman I have chosen to serve grabs Derrida's corpse and urges it to walk with us, back up the stairs. She climbs ahead, tugging the corpse behind her, and I climb behind, looking back down into Hell and up into the dawn light of the City of Angels.

Then we are out on the sidewalk on the edge of Beverly Hills, and the sun is coming up. I offer the woman one of the clove cigarettes. "I don't smoke," she says. Neither do I.

- -

We walk east, down Wilshire. The going is very slow with the zombie Jacques Derrida.

Derrida is talking but I'm not listening; the speech of the dead is poison. I am dead here too, inside Night island I am on a journey, but here the woman has something that I want; I serve her. Without a quest I am nothing, and the message is the journey, the journey is the message, I am a messenger in this City of messengers despite myself...

Zombie Jacques is speaking as we move down the sidewalk: "My love is a curse on your words, I bray the sea, I am a donkey, but the ocean of my spell swallows your feet, and then your thighs, my teeth are my surprise, they're gonna bite off your tongue—"

"Shut up, zombie," says the woman, dragging the corpse down Wilshire, the green dawn sky vibrant and alive, but it is not my sky. My son is invisible, so far above, my body flees to his body, but not yet—

"Los Angeles is getting to me, lady," I say to her. "When's this quest gonna be over with?"

"You said you wanted to help me!"

"I know, I know." My armor is getting heavy. Can't leave it behind though.

"What did you do with her son, Frenchman?" I poke the zombie in the back with my finger. He is still moist.

"I taught him things..." lisps the zombie.

It's coming up on the lunch rush hour and the office workers are filling up the sidewalk, one of them trips Jacques, and he tumbles to the sidewalk, tearing off one kneecap. He has trouble standing back up.

"Your son was interested in reality," says Derrida to the woman, and she bares her teeth at him.

"I'm going to burn you, Jacques," I tell him. "But first tell me what you told her son."

"I am a spell, you see. My words. His words too, if he wants them to be so. Prostitution is holy; you know that. But with my words, my words... he wanted his own private universe. A language for only one man. Such a singularity...is very sexy, you understand. It attracts. He had begun to speak in the language I had dreamt for him—an idiolect for a magician in training..."

"You are a heretic and a beast. I will behead you, you understand? I will burn you in the street!"

"I've had it happen before..." rasps Jacques.

He lurched down the street again and I followed him, still reaching for my sword that was not there. Los Angeles is almost up—

"Where are we going, woman!"

"I can't take the zombie on my carpet!" she said.

"My time is running out!" I shouted.

"Help me!" She stood looking at me and I remembered why, I remembered why I'd come all those years ago, out of the lighthouse, I was almost a boy, a boy in a man's body, I was alone—

"If I serve you longer I will be unable to leave!" I shouted. "You will bind me to this city!"

"Go then! I can handle this on my own—"

I am gone into the dark.

Rushing home.

I am Knight, of Night Island. My quest is victory but I am a lie. On the edge of your lips. I cannot understand it, it is not given to me to understand, but only to you.

Tell me, did I do right? Did I do right? I serve God but I cannot hear His voice...

Chapter 5 - Home

"Tell me, who am I."

She is not speaking to me. She is cooking the pancakes. The sky is dark and I am home. My boy is on the hyena rug.

I remember that my name is irrelevant. I am dark. We are dark matter, perhaps; I've heard of that...

"Will you put blueberries in the pancakes?"

She reaches into the refrigerator and drops some onto my pancake.

Her cooking is warm and delicious; the sky has colors in it now, I feed the boy some pancake and then he spits it up.

"The King came today," she says.

"What did he want?"

"Me."

I laugh.

"Yes. What else?"

"Nothing."

But there is something, I hear it in her voice. On the horizon, over the hills, I can make out, distantly, my old lighthouse; someone has turned it on again, guiding the whaleships.

"What did he want?"

"You. He wanted you."

"He wanted me?"

She goes inside and washes the dishes. And I remember something; I brought home milk; where is it?

It is empty. I see the plastic container on the counter. One or two drops of milk left in it.

But I did not drink it. And a grief comes over me, inside my blood, I must go; but there is no escape.

- -

The Sea of Grass calms me; I have been walking for hours and hours, almost a day. I can hear my wife calling over the sky; I do not answer.

The grass is red and dark dark green, like an avalanche of sound its branches are wordless words, calming my head, filling me with a soft almost-emptiness.

Last year there was a wolf here and I fed it. But I have not seen him.

Why was the milk gone? And why did it upset me? I am getting too old for quests. But I am knight. One does not retire.

Certainly not at my age. I feel old but I am young.

The grass is changing. Thicker now; we may have to cut some of it down or it will overtake our house; already it reaches three times my height.

"Man!" it is her voice, echoing through the Grass.

"What!" I cry back, echoing out the miles.

"Come home!"

- -

I am in our bed. The baby is asleep.

In the darkness I cannot remember.

Chapter 6 - Crusaders

The next morning I hear the horns. I look over the horizon out my window and beneath the black sky I can see the banner, taller than our house, the Red Sun banner.

Long ago there was a Red Sun, so it is said. We have forgotten. I know now why the King came. It is yet another goddamned Crusade. In the name of the Red Sun he would have me slay again; but I will not.

"It is a religious insanity, woman," I say, getting out of bed. She looks out the window and begins to pack our things.

- -

The boy is on my back; his star above, somewhere inside, haunting us, feeding us. My boy will never know a Crusade.

The question is: where do we go.

- -

I head into the Sea of Grass, if only to help me think. I can hear the King's men and their buffoonery outside our hut, now behind us, with their formal declarations of religious necessity...

I climb faster, holding my wife's hand; her red hair still gleams, though there is more grey in it now; and in my own.

My boy, bless him, is still asleep.

We are swallowed by the Grass and I take out my sword and use it as machete, heading into the thicket.

The wolf may help me, if I can find him. I realize, suddenly, that I am now a traitor. My armor, and my life, are forfeit.

"Take off my armor, woman," I say.

"You need it," she says.

"It will distract them. Take it off and we leave it!"

She does. My boy is awake now and starts to cry, I swing him in my arms, whispering in his ear as my wife undoes the buckles round my waist. I feel a thousand pounds lighter.

"What will the wolf do?" she says.

"I don't know. Take the boy, and go. The King will keep you safe," I tell her. We both know what kind of safety that will be for her. Will she choose the king?

But she shakes her head, slowly, and I take up my sword and slash deeper into the Grass, now as tall as the hills, and growing taller, deeper than I have ever been.

When we are in so deep that I can barely see the black sky, I can hear the first howl.

"We must be wolves," I whisper to my wife, and we get on our hands and knees to meet them eye to eye.

Luck is still with me because the first wolf is the one I know. He remembers my smell. Now he can smell my boy. And my woman.

In my mind, I can hear the speech of the wolf, like a tail, wagging, and fur, soft over my skin, and a smell, my gods, this smell, it fills my brain:

"I serve you," I say, and I find myself bonded to the wolves.

My wife looks at me, and I give her our boy. I follow the wolves deeper into the grass, and my family follows behind.

- -

I am hallucinating, I know. If that is the word. Things are thin here, and colors seep through the barn that is the universe, the seams are stretched tight under this part of the Sea of Grass and the colors move through my brain, dangerous, and I sleep while awake, so as to draw no attention.

I am Parsifal but I shall not speak:

After interminable rainbows running through dark grasses we reach a lake and the wolves drink, and I drink with them, dipping my hand into the dark water.

I listen to the air, and to the stars.

Where is the smell? I must track it; that is my mission.

I realize the smell is a castle. Without my armor? But surely—

But the wolf looks at me. I know I have it right. It is the castle. In the Bronx.

Chapter 7 - Homeboy

“We wait here,” my wife says, tears far back in her eyes, our boy pressed against her breasts.

What little my wife had is now taken from her. I should fall on my sword...

The wolf is watching me, panting, standing at the water’s edge

“Go,” she says, and pushes me into the water, and I fall in, and sink as though I still had my armor on, and the Lady in the Lake finds me and holds on to me tight, pushes me deeper, into the lake mud, through the door:

- -

New York.

On Fordham Road foot traffic is thick. I am outside Homeboy 2000.

“Gold Fronts, Gold Fronts. Discount,” says the proprietor, in his huge and puffy white jacket.

I step inside the shop.

“I will have some gold fronts, please,” I tell the man standing by the dentist’s chair.

“How many you want? We only take cash.”

In my pocket I find the money.

"All of them."

"You got it, man."

I will be a homeboy. I will penetrate the castle.

"Are you a Jew?" he asks me.

"I am a knight."

- -

Having arrived, one asks oneself, is this the right way?

Did I know where I was going all along?

Is the liberation I feel only a side effect of some greater terror?

Sex is in the air but fear hovers over the sky. I got a chill up my spine but gold teeth in my mouth; I am grinning; I am Parsifal.

New York knows me and I know it; I've been here before.

Fordham University is down the street, behind the gates, keeping the black people out.

But I'm a nigger now. In my new puffy jacket.

Big Nigger on Campus.

With a fire in my belly and a dimensional gate inside my anus and a home so far away over the sky—

- -

The homeboys dance on the balls of their feet, they're walking north to the D train in their new shoes and I approach the gate to the castle.

"I need to see some ID," says the man in the barbican. I reach into my pocket.

"My letters of authority await me within."

"Nice fronts man. Where'd you get 'em done?"

"Yes, they were provided me at Homeboy 2000."

"They're looking good. But I can't let you in without some ID, brother."

"Is the Lord Chancellor within?"

"Who?"

"Call him up, baby, I have business inside."

The words come to be unbidden; but it is often this way on quests. I march past the barbican despite the guard's challenge; he does not even have a moat.

The guard speaks into his speaking tube and I see the little chariots coming, making a whining noise, over the tended gardens, the golf carts are chasing me.

It is a blessing that the Red Sun Banner has not yet come to this country; they would be laid to waste, so comfortable are they here.

"You're coming with us, buddy," says one of the mercenaries, and I climb a tree, a good oak, and vault from its thick branch onto the low roof of the castle.

"Motherfucker!" one of them shouts after me.

Within I shall find it; the hound's first smell, my mission, and my release.

A stairwell on the roof leads within.

- -

I have never been comfortable around monks. I can see none, but their smell is everywhere. Young people with brightly colored knapsacks move through the ancient castle talking in bright voices, and I smile at them. They fear me and my teeth. This is appropriate.

I am interloper but I will deliver you from evil. For my kingdom lies within my heart and it is both unassailable and borderless.

One of the mercenaries has spotted me and I rush deeper into the castle, fleeing their raised voices and walky-talkies.

I am hunted but I am a hound, my nose can smell the corruption.

I am the K train. Knight originally meant "boy"—and though I be a puppy my teeth are sharp and my loyalty outlives this human universe; I can smell you.

The Jesuit bars my way, under the aegis of his guild emblazoned over the marble arch above him, his arms crossed he says:

"What are you doing here, son?"

"Got a long low rider for you, brother, and I tell it true. These times ain't gonna get us what we need till we ride 'em out; so I'm your charger, gonna give you a pony ride, White Father."

"That's very creative, young man, but our campus is closed to unannounced visitors. Did you sign in with security?"

"I am on a mission from God."

He smiles then, a smile I do not like. "So are we all son, so are we all. But I suspect yours and mine are not so intertwined. Please, the exit is this way."

There is a look in his eye then. He recognizes me. He knows that I am Parsifal! Was he my enemy before? Do I need to slay him? Speak to me, God!

But God is silent.

If you want to ride the K train you got to do it quiet, lull on the ball of your heel and whisper to me the password primeval, not democracy but *fate*, more than three sisters, it is an order of light, a particlewave whose name is justice:

I grab the priest and hustle him into the restroom.

"Your brothers made a mistake," I hiss into his ear. "You may have revived Derrida but Night Island has a purity you forgot, you see? All the old dreams..."

I pin him against the urinal. He is terrified and I see he is wetting his pants. I show him my gold smile.

"Purity is a terrible thing, but we remember it. When we have to. Otherwise I and mine cannot come, you understand? I serve a wolf."

"My wallet is in my pocket..." He is trembling.

"Do you want to ride the K train?"

Someone comes in to the restroom then, takes one look at us and ducks back out. I'm running out of time.

“Hurry, come on now brother, it’s coming,” and I feel the light over me, God, but even more, the Wolf.

The howling is a terrible grace and it feels me with wonder as the restroom fills with yellow light.

“Dear God,” the priest says and I hold the moment in my mind, letting the light slip into my head.

“A miracle,” says the priest.

“Do you hear the rails a-thrumming, priest?”

“Who are you?”

“My name is Dun; I come from Night Island. Though I penetrate your castle I do so in peace and now you must show me the secret your Guild has hidden here. Where is your Holiest of Holies?”

“I could have you arrested.”

“You are a priest, yes?”

“I am a member of the Society of Jesus.”

“Where does your society convene?”

“We live in a dormitory on campus. We worship our Lord there. You would be welcome to visit...we could pray for you.”

“Not where you sleep. I seek the Holiest of Holies; the Wolf knows that you have been—”

The guards burst in then and I find I have lost my dancing shoes. What a thing is this life. I am a blunted sword without even a scabbard who must found a nation for a people no one has ever heard of—

"Havoc!" I cry, and throw myself upon them, and they taze me.

Chapter 8 - Indefinite Detention

I should have used intrigue, not frontal assault. For every fortress taken by the sword, a thousand were taken by a woman's whisper.

I am bound in a white room. In the corner I can see a small mound of fresh shit.

A radio is playing on the ceiling.

"it's such a perfect day, and I want to spend it with you..."

Behind the radio I hear a different voice.

"Sit up," it commands.

I sit up, though it hurts. I can feel the cuts on my back against the tile wall, burning and freezing.

"State your name."

I clear my throat. "Dun. From Night Island."

"State your employment."

"I am a knight."

The song is still playing: *"take me away...out behind the barn..."*

Behind the barn that is the universe. I am lodged in a seam of reality, like a flea. If I struggle too much I will cause a tear. I must be still.

“Who is your lord?”

“I am a free lance.”

“We permit no freelancers here. State the name of your lord.”

“I am bound by covenants. I beg you, formally, take my life or deliver to the wolves a request for ransom; I am in their service.”

“Which wolf do you serve?” says the voice behind the song. The song is saying: “*cut it out. cut it out.*”

I move my wrists behind my back but they are bound tightly with something synthetic, and fixed to the wall behind me.

I realize, perhaps for the first time, that I accepted my service, not just to the wolves, but to my knighthood itself, knowing nothing of what it would mean. Perhaps this is part of the definition of a knight: we do not know what we are bound to become when we take the oath.

“WHICH WOLF WAS IT?” asks the voice.

There is a face in the room, a horrible face. It has no body but it has eyes and I am screaming...

- -

The sea is her hair; I barely exist. Somewhere over the skerries I bank a seagull in the curve of time; I can see her eyes, cut into the cloud...

I am awake. The face had come and looked at me; it was blue. Tell me I did not see it. I did not see it.

Help me!

- -

Who are you!

- -

Can you tell me who you are? Please. I need to know what is happening. Do you know what is happening? I have forgotten something...

A song is playing:

"Somebody done hoodoo'ed the hoodoo man..."

I have a beard on my face. The pile of shit is larger in the corner.

I serve God but first my family. It were better that they forget; let them forget me.

"WHICH WOLF WAS IT?" says the voice behind the music.

"The grey one," I find myself saying with parched lips.

"Which grey one? This one? Or this one?"

They are showing me pictures in my mind. Over on the far white wall, I can see static shimmering on the surface...

"DO I NEED TO COME IN AGAIN?"

"It was that one," I say, indicating with my mind the wrong wolf. Do they read my every thought?

Are you one of them? If you are, if there are factions here, if you have any inkling of what I can do, what I should do, who I can serve—that is what I do...please. Please tell me. Tell me who to swear to and I will do it. All serve God in the end; show me which curve on the path!

"Where were you born?"

The song is saying: *"we are the knights who say Ni..."*

"Were you born in Camelot?"

"I don't remember. Please, can I have some water?"

A tube moves near my lips, moist, from out of the wall.

"Was it near Camelot?"

"I don't know. Water, please." The tube comes nearer but still out of reach.

"What is your first memory?"

"The lighthouse..."

"That would be...this lighthouse?" They flash me an image: broken stones and white flashes on black water.

"I think so...yes."

"How did you come to be there?"

"I don't know..."

"Were you brought there?"

"I don't know!"

"How did you arrive in the Bronx?"

"The wolves sent me. They know something..."

"Yes?"

"Yes..."

"I'm going to come back in."

"No. Please. I'll tell you. I know the wolf. I know his face." I feel them recording my brain, the true image of my brother the wolf, in the Sea of Grass...

"He helped me," I say, "I agreed to serve his pack. There was a smell that interested them...following that smell brought me to New York..."

"What smell was it?" said the voice.

"Lavender...cherries. Pumpernickel. Laundry detergent. And the smell of despair."

"Good."

The tube of water is in my mouth and I can't think because it tastes so good. Lukewarm and stale, the taste of God.

Why have I not been taken away? I have failed quests before. I am always returned to Night Island. My wife, how I've failed you!

"Do you know who I am?" the voice says. It is louder now, the radio has been reduced to a drone.

"No."

"I am your conscience," the voice says.

"No, you're not," I say.

"How do you know, Dark Knight?"

"Release me, sir. Release me and I will let you live."

The voice laughs then, a sound like a wind and static.

"Dark Knight. Now you must serve us too, you see? This is the nature of your being; you are a boy, as you said. If you do not do as you are told, you are destroyed. Do you wish to be destroyed?"

"No. What is your quest, lord?"

"We are interested in this woman..."

Chapter 9 - Los Angeles

It is a fiesta; some formal rite. I am applauding, a cravat around my neck. The officiant at the dais speaks into the tube:

"Welcome to Magic Carpet Con 1435!"

The carpets are flying over the stage. A woman is whispering in my ear, Bologna's mother.

"You," I say, and she looks into my eyes.

"It's the new Tauroid model," she says.

The applause is huge. A large blue carpet, covered in evil eyes, levitates slowly over the audience and comes to rest by the officiant on the dais.

"But don't take my word for it! Let's ask the carpet!" says the officiant, waving ecstatically with both her hands.

There are cheers and the carpet is speaking in its language. The audience adjusts their earpieces to listen to the translation. I want to scream; part of me is remembering. I am remembering why I came, who I am. I am remembering why I became a knight.

In the *langsam*, the longing and loneliness of the boat, I had made a decision. I remember...

It was more than just my wife. Something spoke to me from the sky. Did it lie to me? No, not exactly. But it omitted facts. Now I need them.

I lean down and whisper into Bologna's mother's ear: "Why did I come here?"

I see that she is crying.

- -

In Los Angeles all lies become truths.

- -

We are driving home, after the party. I am driving. The vehicle is a Ford Taurus; I know this. The year is 1435. The Lords of Echo Park have been victorious over the Santa Monica monopolies...we heard gossip a royal marriage is expected.

"Are you well?" I ask Bologna's mother.

"Yes."

"What am I doing here?" I say.

"You were sent here," she says.

I will not think of the blue face in the white room.

"Why here? Your son; did you find your son?"

"He's fine. He's always fine. Make a right here."

I make a right on Madison and cruise by the Devil Burger; its patty rotates in neon under the palm trees.

"Do you want a hamburger?"

"What? No. We can talk somewhere near here. Keep your mouth shut until then."

I do as I'm told. We pass the supermarket and I can see the manager in her green awning, her airplane...do we have enough milk? I concentrate on the road.

"We're going to Elysian Fields," I say.

She nods.

The sky turns from blood to thick violet. Above Dodger Stadium I park the car and get out. I stretch legs and loosen my cravat. Bologna's mother steps out, wiggling her knee as though to make sure it still works.

"We have a little time here," she says. "How has it been for you?"

"I don't know," I say. "I think things have gotten worse. Where is the zombie?"

"I killed it," she says.

"Good." The night is warm. The road is deserted. In the distance I can see an automobile turn slowly through the Elysian maze, its headlights shining and vanishing in the dark.

"I've been sent to spy on you," I say.

"I know," she says. Her face looks so old in the streetlight.

I step closer to her and look at her face. I reach out and caress her cheek.

"I'm sorry," I say. "I am weak. But I'm getting stronger. How can I serve you?"

"What do you want, Knight?" she says.

"Home."

"Is that all?"

"I want to understand."

"That's the problem."

Her eyes seem to be growing larger. The violet has turned to black velvet without stars.

"Get back in the car," she says. "I'm driving."

- -

I remember that I was supposed to forget. In the forgetting, I was useful, I was free. But somehow I had decided to remember, so I became less useful, less free. Now I must decide: what was it I wanted to remember? And do I still need to remember it? My wife is going to kill me when I get home...

I am dark matter. Or mostly. This is why my name is Dun.

I understand that much. But how did I become light?

- -

We return to an expensive house, in the flatlands.

Outside, the dark clouds are talking to one another, and in bed Bologna's mother and I lie silent, knowing we are being watched.

She turns the page in her book, "Dark Avalon."

I am staring into space. I have bifocals on my nose; I take them off and look at them; I have never worn such things.

I long for the Sea of Grass. Now I smell it: despair. And the laundry detergent. Over the central heating.

The wolves knew. They knew it would lead me here. I crawl out of bed and get on all fours in my pajamas, sniffing the carpet. My wife watches me.

I see the dog's face in the wall, pitted in the sound dampeners. Its eyes say I am a disappointment, but they still hope. I can smell on the wolf's breath that my son is well; his star burns over my head, and I remember suddenly the priest in the restroom and I stand, remove my pajamas, and bark like a dog. My yips and snarls slowly resolve into a deeper debate, and then I shout:

"Universe so likely I bray at the sound of your voice because I had never heard it. Announce to me, tyrants, the prelude to the elegy that you would have me arrange!"

The stillness in our bedroom covers my skin with electricity; I listen to the dark.

Bologna's mother begins to speak as though she is reading from the paperback, though I know it is the voice of the dark.

"I thought you were stupid, knight," she says, licking her finger and turning the page, "but I guess I was wrong. What does it feel like, being you? To you, does it seem normal?"

I stand nude and watch her lips move. I say, "Normal enough. Elegies don't ordinarily have preludes, you know. It's a waste of time."

"Yes...what kind of a prelude do you think it should be? Should it be torture? Should it be variegated torture, like fine-grained bacon, with ripples of understanding mixed in with the knives?"

"You didn't kill Derrida, did you?" I say, snarl on my face.

She looks like she's going to cry again.

"I wanted to..." she says.

"I'm getting dressed," I say, and walk into our closet, where I am confronted with two dozen suits all in the same shade of black.

- -

I am remembering. The one thing Parsifal must never do. I am sorry if I shouted at you earlier; I remember now that you are not in control of this. You're along for the ride as much as I am. I wish I had known that earlier.

My oath is a terrible thing; so much older than the universe. I am going to break it.

- -

I have been down below; I have gone down below, underneath my mind, and yours.

I had to know, you see, and in knowing, I am a different man.

Whatever I might have told you; whatever it is that I wanted to tell you, that is no longer possible.

I am a knight and I serve my country, but my family first. My son has a yellow sun, as I have told you, and this is still true, but the meaning of these things must change because I had to know, I had to know what I'd become.

Is it inevitable that we hunger for knowledge and then weep to see the ignorance washed away? All the identity that ignited round the fuel of that beautiful ignorance, a protective shelter, a wake of worlds.

Anyway.

You want to know what happened.

- -

I had to go back to Hell; Derrida was still alive. Or un-alive. Whatever. Still fucking talking, anyway.

Men in brightly colored jumpsuits hopped about on their feet outside Hell's corporate offices, wearing masks and hooting. I raised my hand, as though in greeting.

Underneath Los Angeles, Hell vibrates with its pleasures, sending out the psuedopods of grief and Disneyland that penetrate the consciousness of the continent. And underneath that, in the factories where pistons and vises pound out the shapes of dreams, Derrida stuck his French fingers, little *sabots*, into the machinery of the universe.

Which was all the same to me; I exist in many.

In Los Angeles the people are careful about what they reveal, what they say; so too with me. What I can tell you is that the powers that be had finally decided that they'd had enough of Derrida.

I rolled on the bottoms of my feet in my Italian shoes, grinning.

"Possession may be 9/10ths of the law, but I am the final 10th, boys. My name is Dun and I come from Night Island. I serve the forces of this universe."

"Night Island does not exist," hissed one of the jumpsuited masks.

"Neither do you," I said, "but here we are. Let me in, won't you? Do I need to phone my boss?"

The jumpsuits pressed their skulls against one another, like ripe fruits. One looked over at me with dark eyes.

"Give us your suit first," he said, with a ghostly smile.

I smiled wider.

"How about I just fuck you motherfuckers up?" I said.

My fist connected with his jaw and I remembered why I became a knight. I am a fighter. I fight for you. I fight for justice, though it be untrue, with blood on my hands.

Can you understand that? Can you understand that I serve a lie, and that I know I do, and that I do it anyway?

Do you do any different?

The jumpsuits danced around me with their fluorescent windbreakers and cold ocean eyes and I took out my knife.

- -

To spill blood is to learn the lesson of the Earth, whose lesson is the same as this universe; we welt and wilt and will the wisp of truth out of our cuts, empathizing deeper with each war.

My suit was covered in blood.

Derrida was wrong, you see. Not that it matters now. In the scheme of things he was simply inconvenient.

I hummed a little tune to myself; relieved of the terrible burden of being a Man, now I was only an ape, love primeval written over my fingers.

I know now that the castle is inside us. Though the Jesuits erected their own Dionysian Kingdom etched into a side of their heart, and though the magnificence of their palaces suggests the holy Holies lie behind stone, their true location is within; their guardian: the mind.

In this way self-understanding is a terrible Chinese vise and you doom yourself with every lesson learned. But I wanted in.

Don't you?

I bear a message. My message is:

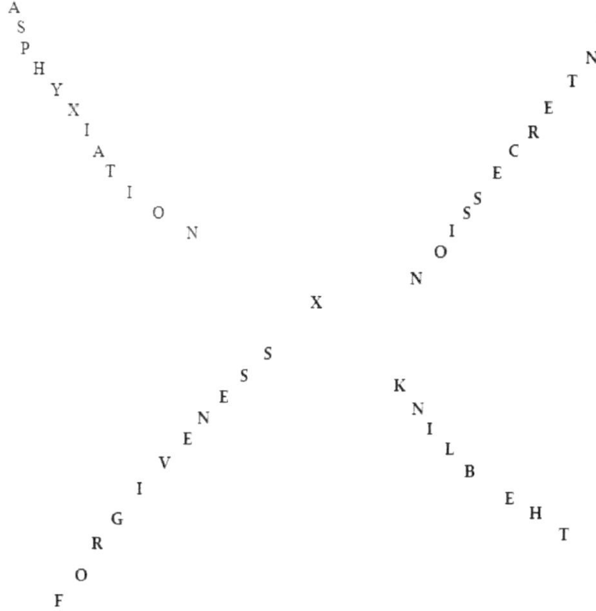

Will I arrive at X? And do I want to?

I am humming a tune; the tune is you. You are my fatal music. I am singing you alive.

I squish down the fluorescent office hallway into Hell, blood squelching in my Italian leather shoes.

Derrida! You are gonna be my little Tonto, motherfucker! And in your impressment may your Gallic heritage enrich your suffering like oak the Bordeaux, like Lascaux your cheese. I will sanctify your arrogance with my whip, and with my lips like razors I deliver you into the castle we hold within, the castle the caste, a circle of fire outside all dimension, pyre sans Brunhilda but painted with your luminous plasma face, tired Vercingetorix, a torch to light not suns but chasms underneath my bones, inside your eyes.

Oh Jacques, if only you had known earlier, I would have given you a boat and set you far ahead, relieved you of your undeath.

- -

I too must die to go to Hell; it is okay, I've done it before. Slowly the air leaks out of my face, and my skin burns, and my hair catches fire; my suit burns away and then my soul, and only my bones step further into the silt of French philosophy, the Nile of the afterlife, churning like a butter urn into the soil underneath the Chumash oaks, down under the roots of civilization.

I am gnashing my teeth; I am howling banshee and moon-King; I am Dark island from Night Island. My wife is Lisle. My son's a star!

I burn yellow and black; I am bumblebee. Can you hear my buzz?

"Jacques!"

But all he can hear is the machinery.

When I was in the white room I became someone else. Someone unholy. Holy means the same as "whole" ; it shares the same root. So I am a partial man. I am a fragment.

Slowly the fires of Hell cool to blue. My black bones harder than diamond, my heart further than it has ever been, my eyes gone and my balls made out of steel and quarks numberless to Man, I am a boy, I'm your boy, your homeboy, for this what a knight is, the chnicht the homeboy, the lad with the dagger in the hall, hungry and lonely for a ruffle of his hair, longing for admiration.

Do you admire me, child? I was like you.

Aflame in blue I step into the factory beneath the earth, where Derrida sits underneath the phosphorous lamps muttering in French and watching data stream over his screens as cloud formations get pounded by machinery, crimson black yellow viridian, ashen gears twisting lives into the shapes we see in dreams.

I smile with my teeth and scratch my skull; it is still whole. It is still holy.

You're a good boy, says the voice inside my head.

"Jacques!" He turns to look. With his zombie eyes and his sad mouth.

"Derrida!"

He pulls a lever on the wall and the glass wall slams down from the ceiling, sealing him in, the witness, and the judges with their white wigs and purple robe are dancing over his eternal grave, and laughing at my bones.

Les skilletes.

I'm a skillet gonna cook ya, Jacques, I'm the *mouton* for your sheep, *the bifteck* for your cow.

I shall eat God.

"What recipe have you brought?" shout the judges.

"*Les escargots,*" I say. "*Avec du jambon.*"

Out of my hands the snails crawl and the judges weep, smiling.

"He is your dinner, eh?" they say.

"Yes, he is my dinner. I shall eat him. I shall ingest the son of a bitch."

"Free me Jacques!" I cry through the glass. His eyes are far away.

I'm pounding with my skeleton hand on the witness stand.

""Non!' shouts Jacques.

I do not have tear ducts any more. I am an aspect of your will. I am eternal. I burn in a night that you can hardly understand. I am Freemason bailiwick and judge, with ritual purity inside my nuts.

My balls are whole and I wear a holy midget o'er my shoulders, a shawl made out of a Gaul.

I collapse and I am reborn, with French man in my mouth.

The glass breaks and I reach my skeleton hand in around the neck of Jacques again, his eyeballs wide and alone.

The judges are gone. I squeeze him around his neck and watch his face turn blue.

Out of the machinery behind us the dreams have turned to watch, the hungry ghosts of so many civilized centuries and numberless aeons, caverns and canyons uncounted, the river—

I chew down on my right finger to sharpen it into a point and when it is knife-sharp I reach it into Jacque's belly.

Raw beef.

With each bite, my flesh returns. I wear Jacques now, zombie mask and cloak, dagger of Peace.

I am shorter now, and fatter. I am French.

My name is Dark Island. I bear a message to you. It is:

Sing for me, you son of a bitch.

Sing, boy, for tomorrow we die at Flanders!

Chapter 10 - Paris

À Paris, je mange. Je pense que serai avec toi, mon amour, au ciel. I am eating and I will be with you in heaven, love. But not yet. For the sky of Paris knows me. I am alone.

I am Chevalier. Sans Cheval.

I eat my *saucisses* in the cafe, under the clouds.

Ten thousand generations and not enough, yet? For I evolve. Tell me, have you seen my son?

I hear he's growing up. I hear he's keeping you warm.

I am from Night Island!

A place I have never been!

(except in love)

- -

"*Monsieur,* everything is okay?"

"Yes, boy, everything is well. Bring me some more vino."

"*Bien sûr.*"

I must go home. But I cannot go home. I must carry home inside myself, a Gypsy.

I must stop eating Frenchmen. They disagree with me. Most strenuously.

I suspect now that the wolves were smarter than me; this is nothing new. The despair was rather something that I needed, not something that they wanted.

Perhaps I will become a robber baron. Have I broken my oath yet? I misremember...

How many masters do I serve now?

It is so terrible, life. Like a dinosaur. Like a symphony that does not end.

"*Garçon*, is there a temple near here? A Roman temple?"

"There is Our Lady, *monsieur.* I know of no other temple."

In the Seine Los Angeles and the Ile de France are one in that old fat bitch the Venus of Stone, her vulva the size of the galaxy, the loosest twat in the cosmos—

Our Lady the Queen.

Do I have a mother?

My mother is dark. I am a halfbreed. I am a homeboy. But where is my homegirl?

I can see her somewhere in the sky; somewhere in the glint in your eye.

I am a French gentleman. I am a whore. I am a weapon.

My mother is dark; like Ing was dark. Like Igor was dark on the Volga.

- -

I am weeping outside the temple. One of a thousand thousand men to have done so, reduced to tears by the shape of the universe, by the loneliness of Paris, by the mystery of the Seine. For though the universe is long, it bends...and the Seine carries me away...

The whore is on my arm. I have money in my pocket.

"Jacqueline, what do you want to eat tonight?"

"Onion bread. Cranberry juice."

Her lips bright, eyes dark.

I am on the stone on the Right Bank.

"I would serve you," I whisper in the whore's ear.

- -

I've had too many journeys. I have been too many men. I said that my mission was meaning, but after every quest all I want to do is forget. Now the waters of forgetfulness aren't working as they should. Parsifal remembers. He must parse, mustn't he? Mustn't I break through the valley, and parse the code to recite the mantra that will deliver my enemies into my hands and serve the greed of my Lord?

And I am greedy for home.

I am going into the woman, going home. I am darkness I am light; I am your deliverance and you are mine—

Shake me awake. Tell me that it has an end. I know it has no end but tell me that it does anyway, for I am mad, and life is so long!

Life is so long.

This whore is my wife.

This valley is my shout. This shout my valley.

My armor is of hair.

I am a boy.

garcon!

garcon!

chnicht!

Chapter 11 - Return to Night Island

I lie in the Sea of Grass. The wolf is licking the tears from my face. I have seen through the veil and this okay; behind it is only a woman's face.

- -

I am a prince. I am a *princeps.* I am a principal. I am the principal of a Parisian school. I am the principal actor in our traveling show.

But not yet. Not yet, not yet!

Tell me, will I see my woman soon? I feel her close...

Class is in session. Are you ready to get tested? I have given you my *jambon,* and now I give of my brain to you. In return, you shall serve me.

You shall take an oath.

Are you ready, boy?

"I'm ready, Dad."

"Are you sure?"

"Yes."

"Your mother dressed you up well."

She does not want to see the boy in armor; she is making the latkes in the kitchen.

"Now you will be a boy-man. And you will have sanctuary here, you understand? Always you will have sanctuary here."

"*Je comprends, Papa.*"

"Don't speak French now. It confuses me."

"Okay, Dad."

"Repeat after me:

[from etymonline.com:

oath
Old English að "oath, judicial swearing, solemn appeal to deity in witness of truth or a promise," from Proto-Germanic *aithaz (cf. Old Norse eiðr, Swedish ed, Old Saxon, Old Frisian eth, Middle Dutch eet, Dutch eed, German eid, Gothic aiþs "oath"), from PIE *oi-to- "an oath" (cf. Old Irish oeth "oath"). In reference to careless invocations of divinity, from late 12c.

promise
c.1400, "a pledge, vow," from Old French promesse "promise, guarantee, assurance" (13c.) and directly from Latin promissum "a promise," noun use of neuter past participle of promittere "send forth; let go; foretell; assure beforehand, promise," from pro- "before" (see **pro-**) + mittere "to put, send" (see **mission**). The ground sense is "declaration made about the future, about some act to be done or not done."]

To promise is to be on a mission. A mission is a promise. Do you accept your mission? Your mission: meaning. Your meaning? The mission.

Repeat after me:

We the people rise above the grass, metatarsals flexing to show us the horizon.

"We the people rise above the grass, metatarsals flexing to show us the horizon."

In order to form a more perfect union between energy and matter, I vow:

"In order to form a more perfect union between energy and matter, I vow:"

To serve God, in whatever form is most convenient.

"To serve God, in whatever form is most convenient."

And to obey my lord, whoever he may be, or may become

"And to obey my lord, whoever he may be, or may become."

- -

"And right now that lord is me, son, so go help your mother set the table."

The Red Sun army is not yet disbanded, but the fundamentalists have suffered some defeats. Technically I am *raubritter* now, Robber Knight. But I rarely rob anyone. My son is fourteen winters. I'm getting old.

- -

A Villain has come to visit; you would call them aliens. But they don't abduct cattle there; their appetites are more diverse. It has been years since I last saw one.

It comes over the grass, shaking its tail, moving on its wheels, its eyes watching the sky, and watching the hut of me and my woman. Our banner announces our heraldry. (Now that I am an independent lord I had to pay a goddamned priest to concoct some lines of descent for my family line).

In Night Island the stars are our friends; we speak to them. I do not believe the Villains do this; instead they treat stars as places, which has always struck me as odd. To us they are people.

My son in his new and shining armor is standing by me on our hill. My wife comes over and says to him:

"Your bed time. Shoo."

"But mom!"

We give him a look and he goes inside to take off his armor. I put my arm around my wife. I feel old. But it is not a bad feeling.

Some nights I still dream of Bologna's mother. Her sad eyes and homeless hair. The Villain is climbing the rocky slope below our hut, folding up its metal cart to carry over its shoulder, its blue legs creaking as it climbs.

I feel like wearing sunglasses to shield me from the Villain's frightening eyes, but I know this is merely a bad habit I picked up in Los Angeles. There is already enough darkness in our eyes here.

"I am a man," says the Villain as he approaches, bowing.

"I am a man," I say.

"I am a woman," says my wife.

"Will you have food?" I say.

"I have eaten already," it says. Its reddish eyes watch the dark sky.

"Please, sit," I say, and we sit on the flat stones in the heath.

"Please," says the villain, and it reaches out one of its blue tentacles towards my wife, and she takes it in her hand, listening with her mind.

There is so much that I don't understand. But since when did knights need to understand anything?

"He's sick," she says.

Shaman again, and my wife must wear the masks. I keep the fire hot outside. My boy goes hunting alone as I chant for my wife, adding to her mantra over smoke. I do not like it but she has done it a dozen times since I married her; she is a healer.

Perhaps a Robber Knight is a more accurate title than I would like. What I must rob now are the roads themselves, no different in principle than the highwaymen of history. I keep certain routes open which means I must close others; I am a switching station and I am a line.

I know this Island must be kept small.

What I fear, even more than myself, is Earth. The fire is hot enough. I must hunt too.

- -

Under the darkling sky with my bow. I need three saints, the size of marmots, little wizards in their rotten logs, peat bungalows. Animals hold so many things; their spirits can be made into paint, like my wife wears on her face.

It has been both too easy and too hard to get to you; now I hope a road will be better.

This line will hold, but if I stretch this telegraph to you, if it penetrates to your awareness, will we still be small enough? Will we still be small enough for what we must do? Together?

I crouch behind a log upwind and peer through my cloak down into the shade where the saint is clucking to itself. I let my arrow fly out from my mind, a series of questions which I hope will kill the little critter quickly:

Are you friendly?
Are you cold?
Are you alone?

I take its life, say a prayer and toss its body into my sack..

The saints, the marmots, are brown and wise, older even, perhaps, than our Island. With three of them I can make the road to you. Erect the telephone pole. Fire the grappling hook into the wormhole.

I bag three of them at last, but I manage to twist my ankle and I cry out, rolling in the heath.

The Villain has been healed; my wife has not lost her touch. He stands over me, his reddish eyes sad. He sees my bag.

"What are you doing?" he says.

"We need a road," I say.

"We have many roads!" he says.

"Not like this one."

"You will bring more like you here," he says.

"Probably. But there's no help for it now. I have made powerful enemies. We will be swallowed completely if we do not make at least one narrow road that leads straight to their world."

"It may be we can't visit as much then."

"That will grieve me. Help me up?"

He extends his tentacle and I hold on tight.

The spirits of the saints, their little furry bodies rustling in the ether, hover over my shoulders. And in my bag.

I am so tired sometimes.

- -

These Gallic galaxies and tired centurions, Derridean envelopes unread sent out between the stars, a small and silent sentinel, Appian Way, I wind and wend, I bind the universe, I say the word—

cacophonous

every dissonance is an insistence and I say, I say, I say:

I spike the saints into the earth, my stakes the swords of melody my hands cello and my eyes cherrywood drum, down into Washing Town, nuclear, charm strange up and down, color of the symphony, Terra and her mysteries—

"What are you doing?" my wife asks.

"Don't interrupt the spell," I say.

"What are you *doing*?"

But it is through. The spell is on its way. The mission? Your meaning? The line of division, Appius, a little gravel and a little stone, quantumly entangled—

"You would summon others here?" she says.

"No. Only an invitation. We have to have it. Or Night Island could be destroyed."

"What is it that you want?" she says. "One of your whores from your dreams?"

"No," I say, and put my arms around her, but she is stiff.

My boy comes running through the grass.

"I got a coney, Dad!"

I smile but my wife is already headed inside our hut.

"Good work," I say, and ruffle his hair, and he looks down at the bodies of the saints and kneels as he's been taught, kissing his knuckles and whispering a prayer.

Saints may you protect us. Make us our Line through the Dark.

Rail on the ship. Mercury spinning—

I am so old now. How old am I?

"How old am I, son?"

"I don't know, Dad."

"Will you fight for me?"

"Yes."

"You're a good boy."

"I'm a boy-man now."

"I know."

- -

These terrible summonings. I have nightmares for a week. In one of them I am back inside the Lighthouse, having never sailed.

My *langsam* is eternal, I think inside the dream. This *langsam* shall never end, O come in my boat, O come in my boat into the shining red sea. I carry only oars and my mind is leaking out into the waves—

I can no longer see the limestone of the lighthouse and the fish are silent and my death has already come or it is coming again—

I awake in sweat.

You have sought us and we are found. We are Night Island.

I bow to you, Visitor.

Will you have meat?

Etymonline:

guest (n.)

> Old English gæst, giest (Anglian gest) "guest; enemy; stranger," the common notion being "stranger," from Proto-Germanic *gastiz (cf. Old Frisian jest, Dutch gast, German Gast, Gothic gasts "guest," originally "stranger"), from PIE root *ghosti- "strange" (cf. Latin hostis "enemy," hospes "host" — from *hosti-potis "host, guest," originally "lord of strangers" — Greek xenos "guest, host, stranger;" Old Church Slavonic gosti "guest, friend," gospodi "lord, master").

O Guest who is a stranger, you personified as Lord of Strangers, How Strange shall you be?

My name is meaningless but my hand is warm. Over here our stars are conscious! You will not take them away. Never ever ever—

Yes, I built that road. Or my saints built it. As they built me. As they squeak us into being. Along the frequency of charm strange up down sad and fire on the mast of ship we wearily slip into the waves again, O Earth—

Chapter 12 - In Orbit

I am like your Armstrong now. A knight serving a wandering star. Of soil. I am hovering over the face of your waters, in my spacesuit.

I remember why I came to Night Island, though I don't remember when. To get away.

Can I keep my Gypsy heart intact?

I feel I see a thousand faces, hovering against the darkness over the blue and white Earth. Amongst them, my wife, with her shining red hair.

I remember when I saw her, gliding through the water on her little skiff. Do I know her any better now than I did then?

I've built a road. To you. Please, tell me you'll respect our fatal songs and our living stars. Things are changing.

Your wandering star, the Earth.

We wander together, you and I, the evening stretched out against the sky and we're the ether, tuning frequencies we hear inside the night—

The holy night—

Listen to the words as I listened to the face of the blue one in the white room.

Though he be horrible. Though we be transmuted into something indescribable. And we shall be, we promise each other that.

Tell me, what now?

In my head, the words:

You've done enough, messenger.

No I haven't.

What else do you want to do?

I want to understand.

But you can't.

But I want to.

What do you want to understand?

I want to understand who we are. Why we're here.

But you've been saying that all along. You're here to do. You're here to do things.

Then I haven't done enough then.

No, of course not. But you've done enough too, at least for this part.

Which part is this?

This is the part in which you die.

Who are you?

We are you.

Who am I?

Who knows?

- -

I am re-entering. I am streaming fire, a meteor o'er America.

I am avatar; descended.

I have a yellow sun up in the sky.

I am a knight and I serve God; my name is Dark, from Night Island.

Here. I am come.

I am your boy. Command me.

Command me, lord!

What kind of command do you want?

A good one.

Now you have built a road. Where does this road lead?

To Night Island. Home.

Who will be your guest?

Whoever will come.

Tell them about it then. I'll get you a sandwich board.

- -

Sandwich boards are out of date; so I accept a fiberboard arrow on Sunset and Vine, "Night Island is Coming," and I spin it in my cuirboulli and my greaves, sweating in Los Angeles sunlight.

"Hey, what's Night Island, man? Is it that new movie with George Clooney?"

I smile and keep spinning my sign, dancing on the streetcorner.

Chapter 13 - Los Angeles

Los Angeles is a dangerous city to have enemies in. I wear my hair and I bear my teeth. I do not smoke.

I am descended. From the sky; from you.

I serve. I am a boy. I have a boy. But he is at home, growing strong, under the night.

I'm getting too old for this, perhaps; but can you get too old for living?

I've been dead so many times. I am alive.

- -

Los Angeles hovers over my skin and I want to weep; I want to scream. So many messengers so little time.

I wear the shape of Jacques Derrida; I seek Bologna.

O Bologna. You and your three beautiful syllables. From the ancient Gaulish word for fortress. Always another castle, eh? We little cave dwellers.

I am headed north on Vermont towards Hollywood, in the back of the bus, watching the yellow light of my son.

We're gonna need some good PR.

- -

I knock on Bologna's office door. There's no answer, but the next office door down opens and out steps Henry.

"Holy shit! How you doin, homeboy?"

"I'm good Henry. Good to see you. Is Bologna around, do you know?"

"Oh man, he hasn't worked here for almost a year. You been out of town, huh?"

"Yeah."

"Well come on in, man! I rent this office these days; I'm a consultant. Come in!"

The seedy Hollywood office in the dim and dusty yellow light feels like home; the yellow journalism and the yellow madness seeping into the blood...

"Thanks Henry."

"No problem! You want some green tea? Carrot juice?"

"No, thank you. Listen, Henry. I want to make a movie."

- -

I'm sorry Jacques. You weren't the man who knew too much but the man who knew almost enough.

- -

What I'm making. It moves; it is a movie. With sound! A talky I am talking I whisper, I sing, I dream a religion I chart the production schedule out in chalk atop the mountain pass, a passable paint job for the roadrunner to run through. I am the coyote—

The trick, the trick is here, so conceal it in your hand, the trump. Trump, from triumph, from the Greek *thriambos*, the hymn to Dionysus—

We're gonna need more bourbon.

- -

The money arrives, but more important, the materiel for my private army.

Our mission: a limited screening. A careful announcement. Dionysus humming underneath the seats, with a little popcorn...

Our war materiel: high definition ordnance, a command structure and a shooting script—

But I am producer, and stand off to one side, paring my fingernails. The director can have the glory and the red carpet; I just want the eyeballs.

- -

Behold: amphoros. Your libation: previews for general audiences.

Dionysus, your trump card tastes so sweet in my mouth. We are Night Island, but *shhhh*, the movie's starting:

Chapter 14 - Night Island, The Movie

We see the hero in his car, smoking, watching the apartment building.

Above, the light turns out.

We cut to:
Darkness, and a woman sighs, and a refrigerator kicks on, and over its hum we hear lovemaking.

Cut to:
The hero's feet step out of the car onto the Los Angeles pavement. We pan up and see the gun in his hand.

Text on screen:

Sing to me Muse, of Achilles and the City of Angels!

Cue music:
The long low beat moves over credits on the bottom of the screen as we follow the hero's feet up the stairs as the music increases and the sound of lovemaking increases until the beat is huge and the woman is cumming and the hero kicks in the door and points the gun in the darkness—

Freeze frame.

Text scrolls over the screen:

What does he do?
He can't kill her.

He loves her.
But he wants to kill her.
But he loves her.
But he wants to kill her.

What does Achilles do?
Patroklus burns inside his heart and in his hand a Smith and Wesson .38...

The text rolls off the screen and we cut to:

The Pacific Ocean.

A boy is playing in the sand. The camera pans up to the pretty blue sky and we see a UFO hover down and land gently. An alien with big black eyes and friendly grey skin steps down the levitating steps and waves his hand at the boy.

The boy waves back, and then goes back to his sandcastle. The alien goes over and helps the boy build.

The camera zooms in to the window in the sand castle:

Inside the tower, the husband and the wife are arguing. They are claymation, and they are angry. We cannot hear their words, but then the man hits the woman and we pan back out as the boy carefully expands the castle, and the alien digs a moat around it.

Title over beach scene with alien and boy:

NIGHT ISLAND

LINE TO NIGHT ISLAND

Am I on an open line?

Los Angeles?

Honey?

The sun is setting and the boy holds the alien's hand and they get into the ship and fly over the waves and up into the sky, out into space, away from Earth.

The alien gestures inside the ship for the boy to press the big blue button, and the boy does, triggering an animation sequence:

À la *The Little Prince*, in simple animation we see the UFO shoot a little sparkling light out of its base which becomes a swirling blue galaxy-shaped door, which the UFO flies through. The spinning blue door slowly closes behind it, winking out like a television dot.

Cut to:

Courtroom scene. The husband and wife argue on the stand as the judge listens from his dais. We see that they are the same couple as from the sand castle.

The judge bangs his gavel.

Text expands over the image:

TROUBLE IN TAHITI!

Text spins in and over:

NIGHT ISLAND IS IN DANGER!

- -

Cut to:

The UFO with the alien and the boy, still animated, swirl over the wine dark waves of Night Island, shimmering yellow wavetips and the black sky—

Cut to:

The hero fires the gun. We see a hole in the wall. The hero fires the gun again. We see another hole in the wall.

Cut to:

The woman, her hands clutching the bedsheet in front of her breasts, confronts the hero guiltily. Her lover is nowhere to be seen.

The man fires into the wall.

Text on screen:

He is thinking of Patroklus.

Cut to:

The woman gets up, sheet wrapped around her, and puts her arm around her man, but he continues to fire into the wall, his ammunition endless, he is firing, firing, firing...

The upstairs neighbors come down to complain, standing in their pajamas at the apartment door, shouting at the couple as he fires, and fires and fires at the wall—

Our ordinance silver made to slaughter vampires, our screen the veil—

Wife. My wife. Hollywood is so tiring.

Cut to:

In animation, the UFO lands amidst the violet heath under the black sky and a man comes to greet them, bowing in his Superman cape. The alien and the boy get out of the UFO and look around.

Cut to:

Courtroom. The judge bangs the gavel. The husband and wife exit the courtroom, still arguing. They argue all the way home along the downtown Los Angeles street.

When they arrive home they go into the kitchen, still arguing.

There is a big red button in their kitchen.

In the midst of the argument they take turns pressing the red button.

With each press of the button we cut to the animation:

A cartoonishly huge and angry looking nuclear missile launches from the earth, shooting through space. We see it nearly hit Night Island, represented as a Little Prince-esque dark heath covered rock in space, the alien and the boy and the man ducking as the missile shoots over their dark sky.

Three missiles are launched over the course of the argument. Finally, exhausted, the woman shouts in the kitchen:

"I'm going to bed!" (we see it as a dialogue card) and she storms off. The man stays in the kitchen and sighs, and hunches over the sink, looking out his kitchen window onto the Los Angeles night.

Chapter 15 - Los Angeles

The movie is only 30 minutes in length and so I institute a confusing policy of instant refunds for any moviegoer who complains (they were told it was to be 80 minutes). The movie is a huge money-loser but I've got my eyeballs.

One of the morning talk shows intimates that I have been threatened to produce an immediate sequel or never work in this town again, but I am enjoying my non-fame, just watching my message trickle in over the airwaves, off the silver screen into the walks and sighs and licked lips of the Los Angeles I'm trying to build, at the other end of the Line to Night Island.

- -

My mission? The movies. But only part of them. I can't stay too long or I will forget I am Knight Parsifal, parsing the signals in the night.

Besides, I'm *raubritter* now, and need to see if I've been extracting any tolls...

- -

Los Angeles is exhausting but I still have money in my pocket; I got to keep a low profile and so I stay in Echo Park, below Elysian Fields, the Greek dead chanting in the night, I buy cheap wine for the libations in the cemetery and I jog in the mornings, over Dodger Stadium, the skyscrapers rising yellow and comical in the distance.

My wife is going to kill me when I get home.

- -

I go to visit Henry.

"How do you take this town, Henry?"

"It's not easy." He laughs. "It's not easy."

"My God. You're a miracle-worker."

He laughs.

"Did I tell you, Henry? I'm not from here."

"No one's from Los Angeles, man. We're a city of strangers."

"I'm not even from Earth."

"There are a lot of aliens around here, Man. Man, you know what? I'm glad you came. It's good to have you around."

"Thanks Henry. What can I get you? How can I serve you?"

"What?"

"I'm sorry...I...I, never mind. Thanks for the drink. I should get going."

- -

I never had a friend before. I had a wolf for a friend. He's still my friend. My son is a friend; and yet he hovers over this sky...

Perhaps I'll never get used to this. Must I swear to never return?

Though I wear a Frenchman's skin I feel almost American.

I know I'm not done yet.

Los Angeles is bigger than Night Island in many ways; and I have built a road here. Through the shifting galaxy our own little road, but solid, still wavering, for those who want to find it...

- -

The reviews of Night Island are terrible so I stop reading them.

The actress who played Achilles' wife keeps me company some evenings; we drink Pernod sitting in vinyl chairs on the asphalt patio behind my building.

"You really live in a shithole, you know that?" she says.

"I know."

"You share a fucking restroom. I thought you were the big time."

"I know," I say.

- -

If I stay any longer I will become a Messenger instead of a Knight; like Henry, I will become independent. I suppose I am a simple man, born to serve. My wife, my son. Our dark sky.

- -

I am leaving. I am leaving you. But visit, will you? Will you visit?

Wherever I have been, or am going, I will feel you. This is what your Walt Whitman said, in the Sea of Grass in the Great Western Desert of your continent, underneath his bootsoles is Night Island, do you see? We are underneath the quarks but that only means that we are you. I am you. Hold me tight, motherfucker, because I'm streaming away—

Chapter 16 - Death

I am dead; or I am dying; both.

Death the door, or this door a death. I die again.

I didn't say the road was easy.

Will you be a Knight?

Will you be a boy? Or a girl? We take women now into our service, on my wife's insistence.

We are building armor to fill the galaxy, a handful of dust, not of fear but the transitory things you feel inside, a moment bright burning in your eye—

My son is grown and still he burns over your sky; I am Dun in darkness streaming—

- -

What is the nature of the Universe? Why is happiness sad? I have put my armor in the basement.

One day a light may shine over our Night Island; but not yet.

Epilogue

The Son's Song

Fill me,
Grail Helios,
Fire me from out your cannon—

Target me, your thought,
Shiver me inside the trench inside your garden—
(the fertilizer)

I am automaton, service *compris*
(we understand we understand we understand:
(for every *cheval* is temporary—

Fill me,
Fair cousin with your grail,
My fire shall storm over your wall,
In High Definition,
My weapon is your voice,
Baritone the throne of our Holy Empire of the Eternal Night
Within—

I am your boy.
Toss me a husk of bread.

(And Make it Pumpernickel!)

Robin Wyatt Dunn
November 6, 2013
Orange, California

ABOUT THE AUTHOR

Robin Wyatt Dunn was born in 1979 and lives in Southern California. You can find him online at www.robindunn.com. You can email him at settdigger@gmail.com.

www.ingramcontent.com/pod-product-compliance
Lightning Source LLC
La Vergne TN
LVHW020047110826
845155LV00029B/669

* 9 7 8 1 9 4 0 8 3 0 0 0 1 *